LOVES DELICATE BALANCE

AN AMISH ROMANCE

Naomi Troyer

Contents

Chapter 1
Mean Without Reason

Dorothy Bowman felt the sun warm her back as she pegged a sheet to the line. Winter had finally succumbed to spring, allowing color and balmy breezes to return to the beautiful farmlands of Lancaster County. Not that she didn't like the winter, she just missed summer every time it left.

A smile curved her mouth as she watched the plowed lands in the distance. Soon they would plant, and new life would rise from the dirt. Over the last few weeks, she had secretly watched every day as Caleb Wanner had plowed the land with the draft horse.

For as long as Dorothy could remember, the Wanner family had lived in the cottage on the edge of their property. Dorothy wasn't sure when or how Mr. and Mrs. Wanner ended up working for her father, but she was grateful that they did. Because it gave her the opportunity to have a childhood filled with adventures and fun playing with their son, Caleb.

Caleb was only a few years older than Dorothy and had worked the farm by his father's side since he finished school. When his father had retired two years ago, management of the farm had fallen to Caleb. Sometimes, Dorothy found it strange that her father owned the largest farming land in the community and yet hardly ever touched the soil.

But then she only had to think of all his businesses in town to know that her father was needed there as well. In a way, it made sense that he preferred having someone else to manage his farm, but the way he managed it made Dorothy sometimes wonder how someone could be so cold and cruel.

When they were young, Caleb was her best friend and came and went from the farmhouse as he pleased. But somewhere between his Rumspringa and baptism, he no longer came to visit Dorothy at all. Dorothy had tried to ask him about it, but he always had a way of brushing her off. The only conclusion Dorothy could come to was that their two years difference in age had become a problem for Caleb. He now saw her as a nuisance, as the wealthiest man in the community's spoiled daughter.

But the way Dorothy saw Caleb hadn't changed at all, or perhaps it had slightly.

She still thought of him as a friend, but no longer through the eyes of a little girl. Instead, she noticed how tall he had grown, how the farm work had broadened his build, and how the sun had tanned his face regardless of the wide brim had he constantly worn. Caleb had become a handsome man, one that made her heart skip a beat every time their eyes met.

At that moment, as if sensing she was watching him, Caleb turned and looked right at her. Dorothy's heart skipped a beat even as her face flushed beneath his gaze. The sound of a horse's hooves trotting into the yard quickly interrupted the moment.

Dorothy turned to see her father had returned from town for the day. Although every store he owned was managed by employees, her father still insisted on going in every single day to make sure no one stole from his pockets and that business was running smoothly.

The buggy had barely come to a stop when his deep voice began roaring across the yard.

"Caleb Wanner, do I have to remind you every single day that if you want to work me you need to care for this farm as if it were your own?" Eli Bowman shouted, summoning Caleb closer with one hand.

Caleb's head hung as he approached the buggy. "I do, Mr. Bowman," Caleb answered quietly as he approached the buggy.

Dorothy knew she shouldn't eavesdrop, but it was hard not to when her father was about to give Caleb a tongue lashing while she was hanging up the laundry.

"That fence, the one in the north field, is down again. Didn't I tell you to fix it yesterday?" Eli continued, his eyes narrow with anger.

"I did, I fixed it. But I told you I need new fence posts. The old ones are rotten and are starting to..." Caleb explained.

"Don't give me that nonsense about needing new fence posts. A gut farmer will know what to do. Are you a gut farmer, Caleb, or doesn't that run in the family?"

Dorothy flinched as her father insulted Caleb.

"If the neighbor's cattle break into our fields in a month's time, it would cost us our harvest. Do you realize what that means? No wages for you for a year! Do you understand me? Now stop gawking at me like I've grown two heads and fix that fence line!"

"Jah, Mr. Bowman, I'll do that right now." Caleb turned and glanced at Dorothy, clearly feeling embarrassed.

"And while you're at it, you can finish plowing the field beside it. I see you only plowed half of it today. You're supposed to be working, not wasting my time!"

Dorothy took a step forward to tell her father that Caleb had been working all day, but before she could say a single word, her father got up from the buggy and missed the step. He tumbled head first into the dirt, landing with a loud thump.

Caleb and Dorothy rushed towards him, knowing that at his age a fall like that could be dangerous. Although Dorothy was only nineteen years old, her father was already in his seventies. Her parents had struggled for years to conceive and had finally been blessed with Dorothy later in life. She had never had the privilege of having any siblings.

"Mr. Bowman!" Caleb cried out, falling to his knees beside her father.

Her father groaned in pain, and Dorothy's heart skipped a beat. Before she even reached him, she knew he had injured himself. He might be cruel to Caleb sometimes and a few seconds ago she was about to defend Caleb against him, but seeing him lying helpless on the ground, she couldn't seem to summon any anger.

Instead, she feared if his injury was serious.

Chapter 2
Kindness Instead
of Cruelty

Caleb had been ready to fix the fence and resign shortly after a few moments ago, but seeing old man Bowman fall had stopped him. Regardless of how mean or how shortsighted the elderly man could be, he had given a home to his parents when no one else would.

Caleb still remembered when his father had told him how they came to live on the Bowman property. The Wanners had never been wealthy folk, but they had been honest and hardworking. His father had worked on a farm as a young man when it had burned to the ground. The owners, not being able to pay him wages, had put him and his wife out on the street with nothing and nowhere to go.

Eli Bowman had taken them in, given them a cottage, and had given his father, Brahm, the position as farm manager so that he could focus on his other businesses.

Caleb kneeled beside Eli and could see from his drawn expression that he was in a lot of pain. He almost reached out to help him up when he realized that his help could make the injury worse. He heard Dorothy's concerned cries and knew that the last thing Eli needed now was a hysterical daughter fussing over him.

"Dorothy, he's fine. But I need you to run to the phone shanty and call for an ambulance. Give them your address and tell them what happened," Caleb said quickly.

Dorothy stopped mid-step. "Is he going to be all right?"

"Jah, I'm sure it's nothing, but we want to be sure," Caleb assured her.

Dorothy rushed to the house for coins before she came out and ran towards the phone shanty at the edge of their property. Caleb turned his attention to Eli again and could see the old man was clearly in a lot of pain. He pulled off his jacket and quickly rolled it into a makeshift pillow before carefully putting it under Eli's head.

"It's not nothing." Eli's voice was tinged with pain.

"Eli! Eli! What happened!" Sarah Bowman came rushing down the porch, a dish towel still her hands as she ran towards her husband.

Caleb turned to the old man. "They can find that out later. Right now I think it's best just to stay still and to keep them calm," Caleb said firmly.

He didn't even consider how quickly their roles had changed. Eli was always in control and now, for once, Caleb was the one taking the reins on the situation.

"He fell; Dorothy is already calling for an ambulance. It's best if we don't move him," Caleb quickly explained.

"An ambulance? Is it that serious?" Sarah asked, horrified.

"We don't know. Why don't you pack a few things for the hospital for if he's admitted? I'm sure you'll want to go with the ambulance?" Caleb asked her, trying to distract her from Eli's painful moans.

"Jah, jah, of course," Sarah nodded, glancing at Eli one last time. "I'll be right back."

She headed towards the house and Eli chuckled before he flinched from the pain. "I never knew you had such a way of delegating, Caleb."

"Hush, just keep quiet until the ambulance gets here. Judging by the angle of your foot, I think you broke your leg." Caleb turned to Eli with a look of sympathy.

"Don't know where the pain starts or where it stops, just know I can hardly breathe through it." Eli's face was ashen, his breath coming in short pants.

Caleb knew little about injuries, but he knew about shock and right now he had a very good feeling that Eli Bowman was succumbing to it.

"They're on their way," a breathless Dorothy called out, running towards them.

Caleb breathed a sigh of relief. "Help will be here soon, Eli, just hang on."

Eli grunted and closed his eyes.

"How is he?" Dorothy asked, falling to her knees in the dirt beside Caleb. Caleb refused to acknowledge how her presence made his heart skip a beat. "In pain, the sooner the ambulance arrives the better. I've told your mother to pack for the night, in case he's admitted."

"That's a gut idea. Daed? Can you hear me?" Dorothy asked carefully.

"Jah, he can hear you," Caleb whispered. He could hear how terrified Dorothy was. "I'm sure he'll be just fine."

"I'll be fine if that ambulance arrives soon. After that, I'm not sure," Eli complained.

Caleb glanced at Dorothy and knew that she needed to be assured. "He's complaining, he's just fine."

Dorothy's mouth curved into a small smile when they heard the sirens of the ambulance in the distance. "They're coming!"

Before Caleb could say another word, Dorothy was on her feet and rushing towards the gate to make sure the ambulance knew where to turn. He looked down at Eli and could see relief in his eyes. He might be stubborn and prone to complaining, but it was clear the pain was getting to him. "They'll be here in a moment, just hang on."

"I can't," Eli groaned. "I'm already lying down."

It was the first time in all the years Caleb had known Eli Bowman that he had referred to humor. It was so out of character for Eli that Caleb couldn't help but be concerned that his injuries included a head injury.

The ambulance slowed at the gate and turned before they followed Dorothy to where Caleb was waiting with him. Sarah had just come out of the house with a bag in hand, her eyes wide with concern as the ambulance technicians began working on Eli.

Caleb stood to one side to give them space, but already knew that something was wrong, when instead of securing the broken leg, they loaded him onto a gurney. He glanced at Dorothy and saw the fear in her eyes. Moving to her side, he murmured. "I'm sure it's just precaution."

"Jah, I'm sure it is," Dorothy agreed quietly.

Chapter 3
Stubbornness

Dorothy couldn't help but feel afraid as the ambulance doors closed with her mother and father inside and drove to the hospital with sirens wailing. She had never felt so alone in her life. In the back of her mind she had always known that she wouldn't have the privilege of growing old with her parents, since she had been born to them later in life, but now for the first time she was forced to face her parents' age and frailty.

She rubbed her arms, trying to ward off the uneasy feeling when Caleb spoke beside her.

"Get your things, then we can follow them to the hospital."

Dorothy turned gratefully towards Caleb. "Denke, I won't be long."

She hurried to the house and quickly gathered her coat and her purse. She took the pot off the coal stove in which her mother had made stew for dinner before she headed outside. Caleb had already readied the buggy and was waiting for her.

Although the ambulance was probably already at the hospital, it would take Dorothy and Caleb at least an hour to get there with the buggy. The Amish community wasn't that far from the Englisch town, but the hospital was right on the other side of town, almost in the next county.

Dorothy climbed into the buggy and couldn't help but wish the horse would trot faster as they headed out of the yard. She glanced at Caleb and wondered if she and her mother would've handled the situation as effectively as he had. Her heart ached knowing how her father treated Caleb just moments before the fall. One day, she wished her father would see Caleb for the man he really was and stop treating him as if he were a no-good worker.

She wanted to tell Caleb that, but knew now wasn't the right time. Her father was at the hospital and they did not know how serious his injuries were. For the rest of the drive, Dorothy prayed. She prayed that her father's injuries wouldn't be serious. She prayed that the doctors and nurses who treated him would be patient and, most of all, she prayed her father wouldn't let his stubbornness offend those who were trying to help him.

When they finally arrived at the hospital only forty minutes later, she turned to Caleb with a grateful smile. "Denke."

"Of course. Kumm, let's go find out how your daed is doing," Caleb said, climbing out of the buggy. He walked around and helped Dorothy off before they headed towards the emergency entrance.

They found her mother in the waiting area, looking slightly distraught.

"Mamm?" Dorothy asked as she rushed towards her mother. "Where is Daed?"

"They're working on him now. They told me to wait here." Her mother's face was drawn with concern, her eyes filled with fear.

"He'll be all right, Mrs. Bowman, I'm sure of it," Caleb said easily. "Would you like me to see if I can find some coffee or water or something else?"

"Nee, denke Caleb," Dorothy's mother said kindly before she returned her gaze to her lap.

Dorothy sat down beside her mother, wondering how long they were going to have to wait. Caleb took a seat beside her and gave her a look of encouragement before he picked up a magazine and began paging through it. Dorothy knew he wasn't reading a single word, instead, he was just using it to try to distract himself from the situation.

She couldn't be sure how long they waited, but when a nurse finally called their names, it was already dark outside. Her mother rushed towards the nurse. "I'm Mrs. Bowman."

The nurse nodded. "The doctor will be out to talk to you shortly. Your husband is doing fine."

Dorothy and Caleb joined her mother just as the doctor approached. Dorothy felt a wave of relief wash over her as she noticed the doctor's calm expression. She couldn't imagine he would look this calm if he was about to give them bad news.

"I'm pleased to tell you that Mr. Bowman is stable and resting," the doctor said evenly.

Dorothy and her mother shared A sigh of relief. She glanced at Caleb and couldn't help but appreciate his presence. He didn't need to be here, and yet he had stayed.

"We've treated him for the scrapes, although I must tell you he has a quite serious injury. Xray's revealed that Mr. Bowman has fractured his right hip," the doctor continued.

Beside Dorothy, her mother gasped. Dorothy took her mother's hand and squeezed it gently for support.

"We have given him medication for the pain and we've scheduled an operation for tomorrow morning. I must tell you that although we will do everything to stabilize the hip without using prosthesis, the road ahead is going to be long. After the surgery, we'll manage his pain, but he will need to stay in the hospital for a few weeks at least. With the help of rehabilitation therapists, I'm sure he'll be able to walk again, but patience is key in the weeks to come. For now, I can't tell you much more, but that his age is a risk factor with both the operation and the fracture," the doctor finished.

Dorothy felt her mother sway beside her and quickly stepped closer to support her. "It's all right Mamm, he'll be all right."

"Here, Mrs. Bowman, sit down," Caleb said with a chair in his hand.

After her mother was seated, Dorothy realized that her father's condition completely consumed her mother, and the farm, the businesses, all of it would probably fall to her to manage.

"I'll check on him in the morning before surgery. There is a pull-out chair in his room if you'd like to stay with him tonight, Mrs. Bowman," the doctor said kindly.

"Denke doctor," Dorothy said on behalf of her mother.

The doctor nodded before he walked away. Dorothy saw her mother's pale color and knew that her mother was afraid her father wouldn't survive the operation. Dorothy shared the same fear, but right now she had to be strong for her mother.

A nurse came to them and offered to show her mother to her father's room. Dorothy wanted to go with, but it was already late and she and Caleb still had a long drive back to the farm. After saying goodbye to her mother, she followed Caleb out of the hospital back to the buggy.

Fear made her quiver with cold and worry as she settled into the buggy. Without asking, Caleb pulled off his coat and draped it over her shoulders. When he gently touched her chin and turned her head to meet his gaze, Dorothy was grateful for his presence.

"Dorothy, he'll be all right. He's too stubborn to let a broken hip stop him," Caleb said with half a smile.

Dorothy returned his smile, although weak. "Jah, you're right. It's just… weeks… Caleb, the businesses, the farm, the house…"

"We'll figure all that out in the morning. Right now we need to get home and you need to get a gut night's rest. We'll come back tomorrow and find out how the surgery went. Right now, everything else can wait. Your daed is all that matters now." Caleb's voice was gentle.

Dorothy searched his gaze and wished she could tell him how much she cared for him. She wished they could be children again without this divide of social standing between them. She yearned for simpler times when there weren't so many complications between them.

Her heart swelled, hoping that one day the divide would fade and she could let herself reveal her feelings to him. She pushed the thought aside knowing that Caleb was right. The only thing that mattered now was her father.

Everything else could wait.

Even her feelings for the man she knew her father would never approve of.

Chapter 4
A Blessing In Disguise

The following morning, it took Caleb and Dorothy longer than usual to get all the morning chores done. By the time they made the beds, the kitchen cleaned, and all the farm chores were done, Dorothy packed a bag for her father.

She wasn't sure how long he would be in the hospital, but she expected her mother would return home today once she knew the surgery had been successful. She also packed a basket of her father's favorite cookies and fruits to take to the hospital.

They only left the farm at eleven o'clock, arriving at hospital shortly after noon because of heavy traffic in town. Caleb helped her carry the bag and the basket as they headed into the hospital. It took Dorothy about ten minutes to track down her father's room. He had been in a temporary room the night before and had been moved to a new room this morning.

Caleb stopped in front of the room and set down the basket and the bag before turning to Dorothy. "I'll wait in the cafeteria or the buggy. I'm sure your daed wouldn't want me here."

Dorothy hated he was right. She hated even more than she couldn't summon the courage to ask him to stay... for her. Without realizing it, she leaned on him since the accident the day before.

But she knew that having Caleb there would only upset her father and after the operation, he didn't need any upsetting. "Denke Caleb… for everything," Dorothy whispered.

As she searched his gaze, she wondered if he felt it as well. It felt as if a current was moving between them, one that was drawing them closer, one that connected them in a way Dorothy had never experienced with anyone else before.

"Good luck," Caleb summoned a smile before he turned and headed back the way they had come.

Dorothy watched him walk away before she opened the door and stepped inside. Her father was on the bed, tubes coming out of his nose and monitors beeping beside the bed. Her mother was sitting in a chair, looking tired and bleak. "Mamm?"

"Ach Dorothy, I'm so glad you came," her mother said with a sad smile.

"Of course, I would've come sooner, but there were chores and… I know Daed would've wanted us to do them first," Dorothy explained, moving towards her mother. "How is Daed?"

"He went in for surgery first thing this morning. Four hours Dorothy, he was in there for four hours. I thought…. It doesn't matter what I thought. He made it through the surgery," her mother explained.

"Any more news on how bad the fracture is?" Dorothy asked, glancing at her father, who was sleeping on the bed.

"They fixed the fracture with some type of metal screws, plates, and pins. He's going to have them for the rest of his life. Other than that, the surgery went very well, according to the doctors. He should wake up soon." Her mother glanced at the bed.

"I can stay, Mamm. Caleb can take you home. I can see you're tired. Did you sleep at all?" Dorothy asked.

"Nee, how could I when… Nee, I didn't sleep dochder." Her mother sighed. "I phoned your aunt this morning. She's agreed to come and get me later this afternoon. As she lives closer to the hospital, I thought it would be best if I stayed with her until your daed can come home. That way I can come and see him every day without taking Caleb away from the farm."

Dorothy nodded understanding. Her mother refused to drive a buggy and had ever since Dorothy could remember. Dorothy herself didn't mind driving the buggy to town on her own, but driving the buggy to the hospital through the business district was a little intimidating for her capabilities.

"That sounds like a gut plan. If I'd known I would've brought you clothes…"

"Nee, it's all right. I can borrow from your aunt until you come see your daed again."

"Sarah, Dorothy?" Dorothy turned at the sound of her father's weak voice.

"Daed?" Dorothy said under her breath as she moved towards the bed. "How are you feeling?"

He groaned with pain. "Like someone took a knife to me."

"They had to Eli, they fixed your hip. You'll be gut as new in no time," Sarah said, moving to her husband's side.

Dorothy nodded. "Mamm is right. You just need to rest and be patient."

Her father huffed. "The farm… the businesses in town."

Sarah glanced at her daughter before turning to her husband. "Dorothy will take care of it, won't you, Dorothy?"

Dorothy's eyes widened. "Mamm?"

"Jah, take care of it, Dorothy," her father agreed before Dorothy could continue. "You need to keep a close eye on Caleb. If you don't, he won't be doing anything of use. As for the businesses…" her father coughed and her mother quickly reached for the water on the bedside table.

"Here, drink this. The nurse said your throat will be scratchy when you came to," her mother explained as she offered him the water.

Her father took a few sips before taking a deep breath. "You need to go every day. Make sure they're not stealing from me. You collect the money and then take it to the bank. I keep the ledgers under my bed. You need to complete them…"

Dorothy shook her head. "Daed, I know nothing about ledgers or businesses."

"You'll learn, you're my dochder and you've always been gut with math. I'm counting on you Dorothy…" her father finished tiredly.

Dorothy wanted to argue further, but realized it would be moot. Her father was ill and in the hospital. Her mother was going to stay with her aunt Ruth for the foreseeable future and it was up to Dorothy to make sure her father's businesses and farm were running smoothly. "I'll try my best, Daed."

"Gut, go now. I want to rest. Start tomorrow, Dorothy," her father said firmly, although he was ill and still coming out of anesthesia.

"Your daed is right, Dorothy. We're counting on you. Here," her mother headed to her purse and pulled out a small sheet of paper. "I made a list of things I'd like you to bring next time. Please tell the bishop what happened and ask him to bring it to the prayer group's attention."

Dorothy nodded, her mind swimming with instructions by the time she went to find Caleb. He was sitting on a bench outside the hospital and for a brief second, Dorothy wanted nothing but to rush towards him and beg him to take the burden off her shoulders. But this wasn't his burden, it was hers.

"We can go," Dorothy said when she reached him.

Caleb looked up at her and concern etched his brow. "Your daed."

Dorothy sat down beside him on the bench and explained to him about the operation and everything that was required of her before letting out a heavy sigh. "Caleb… what do I know about businesses and ledgers? Ever since I've finished school, I've done nothing but help Mamm around the house."

Caleb smiled confidently. "Just because you haven't done it before, doesn't mean you can't. You'll do just fine Dorothy, I'll help you."

"Denke Caleb, but you still have the farm…" Dorothy trailed off.

"Dorothy, relax. I'll help you and I'll make sure the farm work doesn't fall behind. Kumm, let's go home and figure out how we're going to do this." Caleb stood up and held out his hand to her.

Dorothy had never been more grateful for his presence or his support. For a moment, she remembered how much she enjoyed having him as a friend. She knew that this wasn't the time to try to rekindle that friendship, but was it wrong of her to look forward to spending more time with him?

Chapter 5
Unspoken Truths

Caleb carefully navigated through the traffic of the business district. When they reached the edge of town, he could see the situation weighing heavily on Dorothy's mind. She hadn't said a single word since they left the hospital.

He had always loved her from afar, but knew that her father would never approve of a farm manager courting his daughter. Eli Bowman might be a rude and cruel man but he loved his daughter more than anything and he wanted nothing but the best for her.

In his eyes, Caleb wasn't even close.

In his heart, Caleb knew no one could ever love Dorothy more than he did and if the situation gave them a chance to spend more time together, then he only had one goal. To prove to Eli Bowman that he was worth his daughter's hand. More importantly, he wanted to prove to Dorothy that he was the man she deserved to spend the rest of her life with.

"Are you alright?" Caleb finally asked when they reached the dirt road leading to the Amish community.

Dorothy shook her head without meeting his gaze. "Nee, not at all. For the first time, I wish I paid more attention to my father's businesses in town. The bakery, the gift shop, and the feed store are all different businesses. How am I supposed to learn enough to manage them on my father's behalf in one day? I'm expected to stop by tomorrow."

Caleb stopped the buggy and turned to her with a confident smile. "Dorothy, you can do this. Stop doubting yourself."

"That's easy for you to say. You just have to continue doing what you've been doing your whole life," Dorothy snapped.

Caleb didn't let her harsh words affect him. He knew it upset her. He held his silence for a few moments until she turned to him with apology in her eyes.

"I'm sorry, that was rude of me and I didn't mean to be rude. I'm just…" Dorothy sighed, shaking her head. Her eyes pooled with tears, and Caleb wanted nothing more than to pull her into his embrace and allow her to let out all the emotions that were clouding her mind. Instead, he reached for her hand and searched her eyes.

"You're worried about your daed, you're overwrought with the whole situation and I don't think it's the businesses that are upsetting you, I think you're afraid that complications may arise and your daed won't make it," Caleb said gently.

A tear slipped over her cheek as she nodded. "I'm so afraid. I know you won't understand. You don't get along, but he's my daed, Caleb. I always knew that they were old, but I never considered their age taking them from me while I was still so young."

"That's normal Dorothy. If you weren't worried, you wouldn't be human," Caleb said with a smile. "Besides, it's not that I don't get along with your daed, he simply detests me."

Caleb didn't add that his friendship with Dorothy had come to a sudden end on his sixteenth birthday. He could still remember the day as if it were yesterday. He and Dorothy had gone fishing by the stream. They had returned laughing with their buckets filled with fish for dinner.

Eli had been waiting for them. He had sent Dorothy to take the fish inside and start on dinner before he had pulled Caleb aside. The words rung true like a bell in Caleb's mind at the memory.

"I see the way you look at my dochder, Caleb Wanner so I think it's time I made something clear to you. You will never be gut enough for my dochder. I took in your parents when they had nowhere to go and soon your daed won't be able to work anymore. If you want them to stay on this farm, if you want to continue working on this farm, then today was the last time I saw you looking at my dochder with hope in your eyes. If you come near her again, I'll make sure that you and your family have nowhere to go and nothing to take with you. Is that clear?"

Caleb had wanted to defend himself. He wanted to stand up for his feelings for Dorothy, but he couldn't be the one that caused his parents being turned away. Caleb had nodded without a single word and had kept his distance from Dorothy ever since.

Caleb wished he could tell her about that day. He wished he could tell her why he had stopped being her friend. Just once he wanted to tell her he was good enough, he wanted to tell her what her father had said, but he didn't.

Instead, he kept his silence.

Dorothy shrugged. "It doesn't matter now, anyway. You don't have to drive me from tomorrow, I'll drive myself. I know that you're… I know that we're not friends anymore."

Caleb frowned, anger rising in him. "Dorothy…"

"Nee, it's all right. I appreciate everything you've done, but I won't put my burdens on you," Dorothy replied quickly.

Caleb knew he should keep his silence, but he couldn't, not when Dorothy thought she was a burden to him. "Dorothy Bowman, you have never been and never will be a burden to me. Don't push me away when I want to be there for you."

Her eyes widened for a moment at the intensity of his words. There was so much unsaid between them that Caleb didn't know where to start without telling her the truth. Instead, he took the reins and turned to her with a grin. "We'll be the two musketeers again."

Laughter bubbled from Dorothy's throat. "You remember that?"

Caleb turned and met her gaze, laughter gone from his voice. "I remember everything."

For a moment, their eyes met and Caleb wished things could be different. His heart swelled with love for the girl he had loved since he was a boy. It was too soon to tell her how he felt, but hopefully one day he would have the courage and her father's approval to do just that.

Chapter 6
Close-Fisted Old Men

Dorothy had spent the previous night going over the ledgers she didn't really understand before finally going to bed. This morning she had to represent her father at his businesses in town, businesses she knew nothing about. She couldn't help but feel intimidated by the thought.

It had taken her until after midnight to make sense of the ledgers and to realize that her father was much wealthier than she had ever imagined. She had found the deposit slips for each business to bank the money she collected, as well as statements from each account.

For the first time, Dorothy realized that their family was probably wealthier than any other Amish family around. Her father clearly had a gift for business, and she couldn't help but admire him for the wealth he had achieved after starting from nothing but a crop farm.

As she walked out of the house to ask Caleb to help hitch the buggy to the horse, it surprised her to see Caleb in a neat pair of town clothes waiting for her by the buggy.

"Hullo Dorothy. I thought I might go with you today, just to make sure the horse doesn't give you any trouble." Caleb patted the horse's flank.

Dorothy hid the smile that threatened to escape. Both she and Caleb knew the horse hadn't ever given anyone any trouble. It was the meekest animal they had. He was merely using the horse as an excuse to go with her. She couldn't help but appreciate his quiet support.

"That's very kind of you Caleb, denke," Dorothy said as she climbed into the buggy.

"I thought we might start at the bakery and work our way back, then finally stop at the bank?" Caleb asked as he took the reins.

Dorothy nodded in agreement. "Jah, I think that would be best."

A short while later, Caleb stopped the buggy in front of the bakery. When he climbed out and joined her, it relieved Dorothy that she didn't have to go in alone.

She couldn't remember the last time they they had visited the bakery. Usually, her father brought home what they needed. As they walked in, the scent of freshly baked bread and coffee met them. Just like their home, the bakery was void of any unnecessary decorations.

"Miss Bowman," the elderly Amish woman behind the counter greeted her with surprise. "How gut to see you."

"Hullo Petra," Dorothy greeted her with a smile. She'd known Petra for years and the elderly lady had never addressed her as Miss Bowman before. "Please, it's still just Dorothy."

"I'm so sorry to hear about your daed. Is he doing better?" Petra asked nervously.

"He'll be in the hospital for a while, but the doctor assured us he'll be just fine. I'll be stopping by on his behalf until he's discharged," Dorothy explained.

Petra's eyes widened; It surprised Dorothy to see fear in her gaze. "Of course. I've got everything here for you." Petra rushed around the counter and pulled out a few papers. "Here are the receipts for the flour, milk, and eggs that were delivered yesterday. You'll see the cash register matches the amount after deductions." Petra's gaze drifted to the floor, her shoulders hunching with embarrassment. "You can weigh the flour, Dorothy. I promise you I didn't steal any, and neither did the bakery workers."

Dorothy frowned, wondering why Petra would say such a thing. "Of course you didn't."

"Please, just weigh the flour. Your daed weighs it every day to be sure," Petra insisted.

Dorothy couldn't understand why a woman twice her age was acting as if Dorothy was accusing her of being a thief. "It's all right, Petra. I trust you."

The woman looked up with bafflement in her gaze. "You daed doesn't."

Unsure how to reply, Dorothy checked the slips and counted the money before slipping them into a bank envelope. "Denke Petra. I'll stop by again tomorrow. Have a gut day."

"Denke Dorothy. I'll keep count of the eggs," Petra said quickly before she turned and rushed around the counter back to her place.

A short while later, Caleb and Dorothy pulled up outside the giftshop. Dorothy couldn't help but feel uneasy after their visit to the bakery. Why wouldn't her father trust Petra? Had she stolen from him in the past? What surprised her more was the doubtful look in Petra's eyes when Dorothy said she trusted her. It just didn't feel right.

As they approached the gift shop, Dorothy frowned, wondering why it was so dark inside. She turned to Caleb with a curious look. "Do you think the power is out?"

Caleb glanced at the shops next to the giftshop. "Nee, it doesn't look as if the power is out. Let's find out what's going on."

Dorothy pushed open the door and bells jingled, announcing their arrival. They were barely through the door when an Englisch woman Dorothy didn't recognize rushed towards them with a broad apologetic smile.

"Hi, sorry about the lights. The owner is close-fisted with the electricity bill." Her high-pitched laughter showed her embarrassment. "I switch off the lights whenever we don't have customers. Just wait here and I'll go switch them on."

Dorothy frowned as the woman disappeared into the darkness before lights lit up the entire gift shop. For a moment, Dorothy couldn't help but admire the variety of items being displayed. There were nightstand lamps that were so beautiful that for a moment, she wished they had electricity.

"There, now you can see all we offer. Quite a variety, isn't it? I'm Andrea," the woman returned, holding out her hand.

Dorothy summoned a smile, still confused about the close-fisted comment. "I'm Dorothy, Dorothy Bowman."

Andrea's face flushed bright red. "I'm so sorry. I did not know. Oh boy, I guess I should fetch my things and just leave?"

Dorothy shook her head. "Nee, nee, it's fine. How could you have known? Does my daed really complain about the electricity bill?"

Andrea glanced at Caleb before her gaze fell to the floor. "Yes. He says I waste it to keep all the bedside lights on. But how can you appreciate the beautiful lamp shades without it?"

Dorothy nodded. "Jah, you can't really. Especially not in the dark."

"Mr. Bowman has been admitted to the hospital and Dorothy will stop by on his behalf until he is better," Caleb explained when there was a lull in conversation.

"Oh, right, I'm sorry to hear that," Andrea said quickly before she rushed to the cash register. "Here is the slip from yesterday with all the purchases made. You can double check the money; I took nothing. I'll switch the lights off as soon as we're done."

Again, there was the shift in attitude, the air of submissiveness and the avoidance of Dorothy's gaze. Confused, she accepted the money and the list and placed it in another bank envelope.

"You can keep the lights on," Dorothy said, knowing that her father would probably scold her for it later. "It was nice meeting you Andrea."

"You mean you're not firing me?" Andrea asked, surprised.

Dorothy couldn't help but wonder why everyone was so afraid of her. As if she was going to rip off their heads or give them a tongue lashing at any moment. "Nee, not at all. I'll... I'll see you tomorrow, Andrea."

As they walked out of the gift shop, an uneasy feeling settled over Dorothy. At the bakery she had thought that Petra had wronged her father some way, and that was what had caused her behavior, but the Englisch woman had acted exactly the same way.

Confused and more than a little surprised, she climbed into the buggy and prayed that their visit to the next shop wouldn't be the same.

Chapter 7
Money is Power

As they walked into the feed store a short while later, Dorothy felt anxious about how this visit was going to go. She appreciated how clean the feed store was, but found it odd that there wasn't a single customer inside.

A man approached her with a broad smile. "Hello, I'm Anthony. How can I help you today? We have corn on special and weed killer."

Dorothy breathed a sigh of relief at the man's friendly greeting. "It's spotless in here."

Anthony chuckled. "If it isn't, I'll be out of a job. Now what I can do for you? Having trouble with a cow or just coming to buy feed?"

"Nee, actually… I'm Dorothy Bowman. My daed has taken ill and I'll be coming around on his behalf," Dorothy explained with a smile.

Anthony's smile disappeared even as his eyes widened. "Miss Bowman… sorry, I didn't know about your father. I don't believe we've met before."

"Nee, I don't come to town often," Dorothy explained, feeling that uneasiness fill the air again as Anthony's shoulders hunched and he avoided her gaze.

"Right, then you're probably in a hurry to get home. The corn isn't really on special, I just say that hoping to sell some. Sales have been down of late and Mr. Bowman... he says if they don't look up, I'll need to find new employment," Anthony explained in the same submissive tone of voice that Andrea at the gift shop had used.

Instead of taking the money out of the cash register, Anthony opened it and stepped aside. "There you can see everything is there. I didn't take a single dime. The deduction you see on the day's cash up slip is for a refund. I know we don't give refunds, but it was a defective spade. The man nearly lost a foot when the head came off," Anthony explained, rushing through his words. "If you're unhappy about the refund, you can take it out of my wages."

Dorothy looked at him and couldn't help but feel like a villain when she had done nothing at all. "Nee, nee. I'm sure it's fine. If the spade was defective, then it's only right."

She waited for him to give her the money, instead he stood aside, waiting for her. Realizing that she had to get the money herself, Andrea moved closer and quickly took out the money before checking it against the cash up slip. "It looks right."

"It is," Anthony assured her. "Did your father perhaps mention to you about the day off I asked for?"

"Nee, I'm afraid he didn't?" Dorothy said, placing the money in the last bank envelope.

"My wife... she's going in for an operation on Friday. I asked for the day to go with her. Fred will be here the whole time and I can promise you he won't take anything. I trust him. If he does, you can take it from my wages," Anthony said, not meeting her gaze. "I understand I won't be paid for the day."

Dorothy frowned. "Of course you can go with your frau. I'm sure Fred will be just fine. I'll... I'll check with my daed about the wages, but I'm sure it won't be necessary to deduct for the day."

Anthony looked at her with surprise before his face clouded with suspicion. "You're going to take it from my yearly bonus, aren't you? I'd rather you take it now than find out on Christmas Eve that I'm not getting a bonus."

Dorothy gasped at what had happened the year before. "But why... Are you sure that's why you didn't get a bonus?"

Anthony shrugged. "In my bonus envelope was a list of all the days I had to slip away for a few minutes. Like I said, I'd rather you just take it from my wages."

A client walked into the store and before Dorothy could explain that it wouldn't be necessary, Anthony turned and headed towards the client. She stood there, feeling lost for a moment before Caleb touched her shoulder.

"Kumm, let's go."

She wanted to argue with him and stay for a while longer. She wanted a moment to explain to Anthony that there must have been a mistake with his bonus, when she realized Anthony was avoiding her, also just wanting her to leave.

Nodding, she followed Caleb to the buggy. She hadn't known what to expect from visiting her father's businesses, but she never expected everyone to be terrified, intimidated, submissive, and apologetic towards her.

Something about her visits in town just didn't feel right.

Chapter 8
The Devastating Truth

Caleb had laid awake for most of the previous night knowing that today was going to be hard for Dorothy. She had always adored her father and admired him and had never really learned the truth about the type of man her father was.

That was why he had gotten up just before dawn to do everything that he needed to be done to go with her. Although he knew he would never be good enough for Dorothy, he didn't want her to come to the blinding reality of her father's personality on her own. When they had left the bakery, he had seen the confusion in her eyes but hadn't said a word.

When they had walked out of the gift shop, he had seen doubt brew beneath the surface of Dorothy's calm demeanor. But only when they had stood inside the feed store had he realized how much it had affected her to learn how her father treated the people that worked for him.

As a member of the community, Caleb had been privy to more than one conversation about how rude and cruel Eli Bowman could be. He had always tried to shield Dorothy from those conversations. Even as children he had made sure she stayed out of earshot when people were complaining about her father's haughty attitude and suspicion of others.

She was a grown woman and Caleb couldn't help but feel sorry that the image she had in her mind of her father had just been brutally crushed by reality. After stopping at the bank so that Dorothy could deposit the envelopes, he took her home, knowing her silence indicated how heavy this morning weighed on her mind.

They were quiet for the entire ride home. A few times Caleb considered saying something kind, something to assure her that her father had his wonderful traits as well, but he couldn't seem to find the right words. And he wasn't sure Dorothy even wanted him to console her. Her words yesterday might have been said in anger, but Caleb knew they were the truth. He was a farmer, not a business man; her father employed him, not his sweetheart.

So instead he kept his silence, kept himself firmly in the position her father had put him in years before, as a mere peasant in contrast to the princess sitting beside him. It didn't matter that he cared or that he loved her. All that mattered was that Dorothy was out of his reach. Even if he wanted to support her and be there to offer her help, he couldn't unless she allowed him to.

They arrived at the farm and Dorothy climbed out without a single word. Caleb unhitched the buggy and set the horse out to pasture before he headed back to the barn to start on his work when he noticed Dorothy coming towards him with anger in her gaze.

For a moment, he thought she was going to scold him just like her father did, when he saw the tears shining in her eyes. "What happened today, Caleb? I thought everyone in town adored my father. I thought they were grateful for the jobs he's given them, the opportunities… Instead, it's as if everyone hates him. It's as if they're afraid of him. They detest him, Caleb. Once they learned who I was, they detested me as well. How does he treat them if they act like that?"

Caleb didn't answer, knowing that she knew the answer. Instead, he waited for her to finish ranting, knowing that she needed to get it off her chest.

"He treats them as if they're nothing. As if they don't make a difference to him. Instead of being kind and grateful for all the work they put in, he accuses them of stealing, takes away their bonuses because they care for their families…. I never realized he could be that mean. I've seen him scold you and I just thought it was because you didn't get along, but now…" a tear slipped over her cheek as she shook her head. "They hate him, Caleb. They hate me just for being his daughter. Is it just them… or is there more?"

Caleb shrugged and took a step towards her. "Dorothy, your daed isn't a kind man. Everyone respects him but that doesn't mean they… like him."

"They respect him because he has money, don't, they? They respect him because he holds their livelihoods in their hands. Even the people that don't work for him…. The other farmers, quilters… the entire community, because they depend on his shops, on his business. I never considered that the reason we don't have many people over was because of this. I simply believed what my daed told me. That our family was enough." She was all but sobbing now.

Caleb couldn't just stand there and watch her cry. For Dorothy, today had been like learning that the sky wasn't there and she had been stuck inside a blue box her entire life. He moved towards her and pulled her into his embrace. Caleb felt her body shiver with sobs against his shoulder as he held her. He let her cry until the tears finally stopped.

When she stepped back, she searched his gaze. "You knew, didn't you? You knew how mean he was and you never told me?"

"Dorothy… what did you want me to say? It wasn't my place."

She let out a sigh. "You're probably right, I just… I can't believe the type of man he is. He's always been kind with me. He's never aimed a harsh word in either me or my mamm's direction. I thought that was the kind of man he was."

"That's because you and your mamm mean everything to him," Caleb explained.

"And they mean nothing but profit," Dorothy said, understanding.

Caleb smiled at her with apology in his eyes. "I'm sorry, Dorothy. I know how hard this must be for you."

"How can I manage these businesses when they hate me? They don't want me there. They think I'm just like him," Dorothy whispered.

Caleb tilted her chin to meet his gaze. "Then show them you're not. Show them that a Bowman can be kind and understanding. Show them they matter and that they're appreciated. Treat them like they deserve, Dorothy, not like your daed. You're a gut person and the best thing you can do is just to be yourself."

Dorothy sighed heavily. "Denke Caleb. For yesterday, the day before, today, I don't know how I would've managed without you."

Caleb felt his heart skip a beat. Did she just admit that she needed him, or was he imagining it? "You know I'll always be here for you, Dorothy. You just have to ask. If you need help to put everything into the ledgers tonight, don't hesitate to ask."

Dorothy smiled through the devastation in her eyes. "Denke Caleb. You're a gut person too. I'm sorry my daed doesn't see that."

Her words made Caleb's throat clog with emotion, but before he could respond, she turned and headed back towards the house. As he watched her walk away, Caleb couldn't help but feel hopeful that while Eli was in the hospital, he might just win Dorothy's heart.

Chapter 9
Improvement Beyond Expectation

Over the next few weeks, Dorothy did exactly what Caleb suggested. She treated the managers of the shops in town with respect and trust. She had figured out the ledgers and had kept track of the shops' incomes the year before and the current year. She was surprised to see that with every passing year, the profits on the stores had been steadily declining.

She couldn't help but wonder if her father's treatment of his employees wasn't contributing to the decline in profit. Intent on turning things around and getting the managers to not only trust her but to look forward to her visits, she began making slight changes.

She spent two days at the bakery to learn how much flour, eggs, and other ingredients were necessary to bake all the daily items. Once she had all her weights and measurements, she had gone back over the ledgers, only to realize there had never been discrepancies when she compared them to the number of sales.

The days the ingredients were missing were days the bakery had taken in extra orders that hadn't been planned.

Her father's accusations were wrong and to suspect someone as if they were a thief and to treat them as such was a terrible thing to do.

Next, she focused on the gift shop. She insisted the power remain on at all times and with the nightstand lamps on; it lured people in from the sidewalk, which caused a spike in sales. Dorothy went even further and requested the electricity usage of the other shops surrounding the gift shop, only to learn that the gift shop's power usage was completely within bounds. Her father had the store sitting in the dark for no reason.

After the first three weeks, she quickly saw that the number of sales completely outweighed the savings on electricity.

Her next focus was the feed store. Once Anthony came to feel easier around her, he finally told her that the previous manager had stolen from the cash register. That was why her father constantly accused him of doing the same.

Instead of suspecting Anthony like her father had done from the start, Dorothy trusted him. Because he was such a good salesman, she tried to run a weekly special by actually discounting a few items every week. The sales at the feed store improved just as did Anthony's treatment of her.

After visiting her father in the hospital on a Saturday morning, she and Caleb arrived home just after noon. As it was Saturday, Caleb had the afternoon off until the evening chores would begin. Dorothy expected him to head to his family's cottage at the edge of the property, but instead, wanted to enjoy his company a little more.

She helped him unhitch the horse and told him of the changes she had made and the improvements she had seen. For some reason, Caleb's approval had become more important to her than her father's.

When she'd been at the hospital, she had considered discussing the changes with her father and had decided against it. Her father was improving, and the rehabilitation was moving along at a steady pace. His age counted against him, but he still soldiered ahead. The last thing Dorothy wanted was to upset him by telling him about all the changes she had made. Not only would her father be furious, but it might cause a delay in his recovery. So instead, she pretended to do everything like he had asked.

When she finished telling Caleb about the profits improving and how Anthony now invited her to stay for coffee whenever she stopped by, Caleb's mouth curved into a smile.

"I always knew you were a gut woman, Dorothy. now I know you're wunderbaar in business. I've heard from a few other people how much your influence has brought hope back to the community. Instead of avoiding the Bowmans, everyone is eager to see you at church," Caleb said with a proud smile.

Dorothy beamed beneath his approval. "Really? I don't think my daed is going to be thrilled, but I am. It isn't right the way he treated them. And I'm proving that you don't need to be mean or rude; the businesses are doing better than ever."

Caleb nodded. "Exactly."

Their gazes met and held for a moment and Dorothy couldn't help but wonder how much longer she was going to hide her feelings for Caleb. With every passing day, they just became stronger, and moments like now just made her realize she was falling deeply in love with a man who used to be her best friend.

Just another thing she knew her father wouldn't approve of.

For a moment, they both just stood there and Dorothy wondered if Caleb felt it as well. Did he feel the way the air seemed to grow heavy between them with unspoken words? She wanted so much to ask him if he felt it as well, but she held her silence.

Because if she asked and he told her he didn't feel the same way, Dorothy wasn't sure if she could survive the disappointment. Right now she could hope that he did and she could secretly dream of a future with him.

For now, that had to be enough.

Besides, she had her father's businesses to focus on.

Chapter 10
A Plain Man's Fortune

Caleb couldn't help but be proud of the progress Dorothy had made over the last few weeks. He had known from the beginning that she could handle the challenge of managing her father's businesses. He just hadn't realized how good she would be at it.

He heard not only from his parents but from other members in the community how well she was doing. She had breathed new life into businesses that had only been supported in the past because there hadn't been any other options. Now, people willingly supported the bakery, the gift shop, and the feed store. The discounts had made people once again favor the feed store and as for the bakery, with a friendlier atmosphere in store, the orders had been selling better than they had in the months before.

It warmed Caleb's heart to see Dorothy flourish under the pressure. He had always known she wasn't like her father, cruel and cold, but he couldn't help but be amazed by the woman she had become. She was confident of her decisions and treated the employees with care and trust, making a difference he hadn't even known would be possible after so many years beneath Eli's hard hand.

But the problem was, the more he admired what she was doing, the more Caleb fell in love with her. His feelings for her had never been more pronounced than they were now. It also didn't help that he saw her so often. In the past, he had barely spoken to her, but now, they spoke almost every day.

He had just finished for the day and arrived at the cottage he shared with his parents when the scent of shepherd's pie met him on the porch. His stomach grumbled at the scent of his favorite dish as he pushed open the door.

"Mamm, you've outdone yourself," Caleb said warmly as he found his mother in the kitchen.

"You've been working so hard, I thought I'd spoil you a little," Susanna Wanner said with a smile for her only son. "I made some for Dorothy as well. Would you mind terribly walking all the way back to the farmhouse to take it to her?"

Caleb's heart swelled with love for his mother. She might be a plain woman of simple means, but she had a heart of gold. "Of course."

"Your daed and I were in town today. Stopped by the bakery," Susanna said as she began filling a plate for Dorothy. "They added donuts to the menu. I couldn't help myself."

Caleb laughed. "Dorothy mentioned some changes, I didn't realize they added to the menu as well."

"They did. And as for the gift shop, I just had to step inside after seeing the beautiful bedside lamps. I noticed there was a sign that they need more quilters..."

Caleb's breath caught. "Are you going to quilt for the gift shop?"

"I'm not sure if I'm gut enough. I thought I might…" Susanna's voice held an edge of uncertainty.

"Mamm, your quilting is more than gut enough. Have you spoken to Dorothy yet?"

"Nee, nee. I must first think this through," Susanna hedged.

"I'll talk to her for you," Caleb said with a smile. "I'll be back soon."

As he walked back to the main house, Caleb couldn't help but admire Dorothy even more. By involving more members of the community in the gift shop, Dorothy had unknowingly given his mother an opportunity as well. As he walked, he wondered if Dorothy even knew of all the good she had done.

She was sitting on the porch when he arrived and for a moment, Caleb stopped and just looked at her. How much he wished he could sit down beside her and watch the sunset, to discuss their day as if there wasn't a divide and unspoken feelings between them.

Over the last few weeks, he had wondered a couple of times if Dorothy felt the connection between them as well, but he was too afraid to ask. He knew her father would never approve of him, and even if he did, Caleb wasn't even sure if Dorothy felt the same way about him.

So instead, he kept a little distance, just enough for him to be close to her without scaring her away.

"Caleb?" Dorothy called from the porch when she spotted him.

Caleb held up the plate of food. "Mamm sent you dinner."

Dorothy's smile was honest and bright. "Your mamm is a saint. My stomach's been grumbling but after a busy day in town I just didn't have the energy to go and cook for myself."

Caleb laughed as he approached the porch. "Now you don't have to. Actually, Mamm and I were just talking about you. About all the gut you've been doing."

Dorothy's face pinked a little as she shook her head. "Ach, I wouldn't put it like that."

"Bringing life back into the bakery, weekly specials at the feed store, encouraging local talent to sell their crafts at the gift shop–that's gut, Dorothy," Caleb insisted.

She thought for a moment before she smiled at him. "Denke Caleb. I don't think I would've done any of it if you hadn't believed that I could."

"Nee, Dorothy, you did this. You should be proud of yourself. I'm sure your daed is too."

Dorothy flinched. "I haven't exactly told him. I thought perhaps when he's better…"

Caleb nodded, understanding. Dorothy's father was a hard man at the best of times. He couldn't imagine him now. "That might be wise. Even so, I want you to know…." Caleb almost said the words he had promised to keep to himself. "That I'm proud of you."

"Denke Caleb," Dorothy smiled warmly.

For a moment, as dusk settled over the horizon, their gazes met. Her eyes flickered with interest and emotion and if Caleb had any doubts about whether she felt it as well, they evaporated now into the evening air.

Dorothy felt it as well, but just like Caleb, she was too terrified of her father to acknowledge the connection between them. He took a step back, knowing that regardless of how Dorothy felt, her father would never approve of a courtship between them.

Dorothy would always be the precious daughter, heir to a plain man's fortune. And Caleb would always be the farm manager's son, a man with nothing to offer but love.

For a man like Eli Bowman, that would never be enough.

As Caleb looked into Dorothy's eyes, he wondered if it would be enough for her.

Chapter 11
Prayers of Hope

Dorothy's heart was racing in her chest, flooded with love and all kinds of unexpected emotions, as Caleb stood before her. Just like with her father's treatment of his employees in town, Dorothy knew his treatment of Caleb was wrong.

The whole time her father had been in the hospital, Caleb had done everything to ensure the farm was up to date on chores and other tasks that needed to be done. Although the farm didn't belong to him, Caleb treated it as if it were his own.

She remembered her father's harsh words moments before his accident and wished that she had the courage to tell him that no other farm manager would've worked as hard as Caleb. No one else would've treated their farm as if it were his own.

No one else would've believed that she could manage three businesses successfully.

But Caleb did.

It was his faith in her that drove her to improve the businesses and the attitudes of their employees. She appreciated him more than he would ever know.

It wouldn't be appropriate, but regardless, a smile curved her mouth as an idea formed in her mind. "Would you like to join me for some tea, Caleb? I was just about to make some?"

Dorothy could see the surprise in his eyes. Although they had ridden to town many times alone and had uncountable conversations without supervision since her father's accident, inviting him to tea wasn't really appropriate. He hesitated for a few seconds before the corners of his mouth lifted.

"My throat is a little dry."

Dorothy smiled, hoping that he wasn't just staying because of thirst. She excused herself and went inside to make the tea. When she returned, he was sitting on a rocking chair, gently rocking back and forth.

"I always wondered what it would feel like sitting here, with the entire farm in the distance," Caleb mused, almost to himself.

The cottage where the Wanners lived had hardly any view at all, Dorothy realized for the first time. She set down the tea tray and took a seat. "It is a beautiful view. Every time I sit here, I can't help but be grateful for the magnificence of Gott's creation. I'm in awe of it, regardless of the season."

"Spoken like a farmer's dochder," Caleb smiled at her.

The mention of her father made Dorothy's smile fade. She was her father's daughter and would always love him, but she never wanted to be like him. If the last few weeks had taught her anything, it was that her father's treatment of others was testimony to how he had allowed pride, greed, and vanity to become paramount in his life instead of his faith.

"Dorothy? I'm sorry, did I say something wrong? You seem upset?" Caleb asked, turning to her with a concerned look.

Dorothy sighed, shaking her head. "Nee, nee. It's not you. I just... I can't help but hope that I never become like my daed. It feels so terribly wrong to admit that, but it's true," she admitted quietly.

Caleb's eyes held no judgment. Instead they held understanding as he met her gaze. "Perhaps you should instead try to help your daed become more like you."

Dorothy smiled and wondered if she would ever be lucky enough to gain Caleb's interest. He might be her father's employee, a man of little means, but in her heart of hearts she knew that the woman who became his wife would truly be blessed.

She couldn't help but hope that it was her.

He was kind and generous, and more importantly, he had a way of encouraging her to be the best version of herself. When she was with Caleb, she felt like a better woman, a better friend, and a better daughter. She just didn't know if her father would ever understand that.

They drank their tea and talked a little more about the farm, the weather, and her father's recovery, steering clear of deeper conversations. Dorothy was grateful for the change in conversation, because she was afraid if they continued, she would've stepped across the line and admitted her feelings to him.

By the time Caleb left, Dorothy knew she had a lot of praying to do. She wanted to thank the Lord for bringing a man like Caleb into her life. For having him to support and believe in her. And then she needed to pray for her father's redemption.

After changing into her nightclothes, she kneeled before her bed and talked to the Lord as if he were a good friend. One that understood, one that had the power to change her life.

"Dear Gott, denke for all the blessings you have given me. Denke for a home, a life of gut means, and for loving parents. Denke for sending me a friend like Caleb to sweeten my childhood years. Denke for returning his friendship to me now and for allowing his faith in me to drive me to do better. Bless him for his hard work and his gut heart, Gott. Bless him for believing me, for supporting me and for being a friend I know I can rely on. Gott, if it is your wish, please help me repay his kindness. I love him, Gott, but I know my daed will never approve.

Gott, please help my daed see the error of his ways. Please let him realize that his greed for wealth and his pride have driven him further and further from his community. Help him realize we were all created equal and that no amount of wealth places him above others in your eyes. Guide him back to your gracious mercy, Gott, and forgive him for his sins of the past. Help him see we can achieve more with kindness and trust that we can with cruelty and condemnation. Gott, heal not only his injuries, but heal his heart. I beg this of you, Gott. Help him see Caleb like I do, for the man he truly is.

Lastly... Gott, if Caleb is the man you have planned for my future, then guide us Gott. Help us explore our feelings without my father's disapproval. I beg of you, Gott.

If Caleb doesn't feel the same way, Gott, then I ask of you to remove these emotions and help me learn to accept him only as a friend.

Amen."

When Dorothy finally fell asleep, she dreamed of a future with Caleb on the very farm where they had lived, divided for all these years.

Chapter 12
A Friendship Rekindled

A few days later, Dorothy returned from her daily visits to the businesses in town when she saw Caleb in the West field replacing the droppers for the fencing. A frown creased her brow, remembering how he had mentioned it to her father and how her father had dismissed the suggestion.

Her eyes narrowed, remembering how her father had gone on about the cost of new fence posts and wondered where Caleb had got the money. Feeling concerned and a little confused, she drove the buggy towards the house. She unhitched the horse herself and set it out to pasture before she headed inside to record the day's takings in the ledgers.

A few hours later, when she heard a scuffle outside, she saw Caleb feeding the chickens. She didn't want to be like her father and question his every move, but she needed to know where he had found money for the new fence posts when her father had deliberately said he would not replace them.

"Hullo Caleb," Dorothy called out as she walked down from the porch.

Caleb turned to her with a bright smile. His hair was windblown from spending the day in the field, his shirt scuffed with dirt from the work. Regardless of his disheveled appearance, he made Dorothy's heart skip a beat. "Dorothy! Hullo!"

She watched as he tossed the rest of the corn to the chickens before dusting his hands on the seat of his pants. The chickens scurried towards the feed as Caleb walked away from them.

It sometimes amazed Dorothy how such small things like chickens swarming towards corn could make her heart lift and a smile curve her mouth. As Caleb approached her, she remembered her reason for calling him.

"I see you replaced the fence posts?" Dorothy said, trying not to sound accusing.

Caleb nodded. "Jah, I know your daed doesn't agree, but the old ones were rotten. It doesn't help to keep pulling up the fence when a brisk breeze will just blow it over again."

Dorothy nodded, unsure of how to question him about the money.

Caleb chuckled and shook his head. "Dorothy, if you're wondering how I paid for them, don't. I wouldn't spend the farm's money without you or your father's permission."

"But then…" she hated she sounded like her father, or at least thought the way he did.

"A friend of mine was removing a fence between paddocks. In exchange for helping him, he gave me the fence posts. They're not new, but they're sturdy and still strong," Caleb explained easily.

Dorothy shook her head in awe of him. It wasn't his property, or his responsibility, and yet he had exchanged labor for new fence posts for their farm. How many times did he do things like that to take care of the farm to avoid her father's arguments or wrath?

"That was kind of you, Caleb. I... I'm sure my daed would be grateful," Dorothy said, knowing it was a lie.

"He'd rather scold me and tell me he doesn't need charity, but I appreciate your gratitude," Caleb said easily. He glanced over the landscape before meeting her gaze again. "Although this isn't mine, it's part of me. I grew up on this soil, learned everything I could about how the dirt could nourish a new crop... I know your daed doesn't think so, but this farm is as much a part of me as the breath that I take."

Dorothy felt her heart expand as she listened to him speak. Her father had underestimated Caleb and suddenly she couldn't help but feel even more ashamed of the way her father had treated him in the past. "Caleb... how many times in the past have you–exchanged labor for something else?"

Caleb shrugged. "Don't worry about it. I don't."

"Nee, I want to know," Dorothy said curiously. "I won't tell my daed, I just... I'm curious."

"Last year, the barn roof had a leak. I had a friend come and help me repair it in exchange for helping him plow a few fields." Caleb sighed. "I will not list the number of times I've done things without talking to your daed, Dorothy."

"That's not why I asked," Dorothy said, stepping closer. "I only asked because I realize now how undervalued you are by him. I can't help but feel as if my daed was constantly complaining and yet he never noticed how much you do. It's as if he would rather scold you for not watering the chickens instead of thanking you for getting the feed out of the rain."

Caleb laughed. "Something like that. But I've gotten used to it."

"That's just the point Caleb, you shouldn't get used to the way he treats you. It isn't right." Dorothy sighed and shook her head. "I can't remember him being rude to you when we were kinner…"

For a moment, Caleb was quiet. "And then we grew up."

"But we used to be friends. And now… before my daed got hurt, we barely spoke at all. What happened, Caleb?" Dorothy asked, searching his gaze.

Caleb sighed. "Dorothy, things changed. We changed. We grew up."

"That doesn't mean we had to stop being friends," Dorothy whispered.

"Perhaps… perhaps we can be friends again?" Caleb asked quietly.

For a moment, the rest of the farm disappeared. The sounds of the birds chirping in the distance, the wind rustling the leaves of the trees, and even the sound of the chickens happily clucking as they ate all disappeared.

It was just the two of them. And although Dorothy felt overjoyed by his question, she couldn't help but hope that they could be more. She wanted to go on buggy rides and picnics with Caleb. She wanted to learn more about the type of man he had become and most of all, she wanted to spend time with him without feeling guilty for enjoying it.

But perhaps being friends again would be a start.

It would be a new beginning for a childhood friendship that had been long forgotten. Perhaps if she agreed to be his friend again, in time he might realize that she wanted more.

But for now, being his friend was a step in the right direction, a direction Dorothy had avoided for years beneath her father's firm hand. Although she knew her father might not approve, it felt right.

A smile curved her mouth as she stuck out her hand. "I'd like that very much, friend."

Caleb laughed as he shook her hand. His hand was warm and strong over hers, reminding her what it had felt like when he'd held her for just a few moments after her father's accident.

Caleb might not realize it, but Dorothy already vowed that she would never let her father, life, or anything else impede her friendship with Caleb.

Chapter 13
The Return of Negativity

It had been six weeks since her father had been injured and although Dorothy knew the ledgers were totaled at the end of each month, she couldn't stop herself from making a comparison to the last six weeks compared to the same six weeks the year before.

After a quick ride into town to stop by all the businesses, she had returned home just before noon. On a whim, she had surprised Caleb with lunch in the field before she returned to the house to go over the ledgers.

It was late afternoon, and the day was winding down and instead of feeling apprehensive about going into town again tomorrow, like she had that first week when her father was in hospital, Dorothy looked forward to it.

Every day brought a new challenge, a new story from the bakery, and new crafts to consider for the gift shop. She had never realized how much she would enjoy being involved in her father's businesses, or that she had a natural affinity for it.

When she calculated the totals of each business's profit they had brought in over the last six weeks, less expenses, a frown creased her brow. Dorothy erased her calculations and began again. She redid them for each business about four times before she finally accepted that she wasn't making a mistake.

The totals were correct.

When compared to last year over the same period, Dorothy had showed an increase of almost 50% profit. It was hard to believe that the difference was so big, especially considering she had discounted prices at the feed store, kept the lights on at the gift shop, and had added to the inventory of the bakery.

A satisfied smile curved the corners of her mouth at the result. Because improving profits hadn't been her goal at all. When she had taken over her father's affairs, she had merely intended to keep everything going while he was in the hospital. She could've never imagined that a change in treatment and a friendly smile would not only increase business but improve their profits.

Happily surprised, she stood up to reward herself with a cup of sweet tea when she heard a car outside. Dorothy glanced out the window and couldn't stop her eyes widening with surprise when she saw an Englischer get out before he opened the rear door. Her mother climbed out and before Dorothy could stop herself, she was out the door and down the steps, rushing towards her mother.

Her first thoughts were that her father had passed. Why else would her mother pay an Englisch driver to bring her home, why else hadn't Dorothy known that her mother was coming?

"Mamm? Mamm? What happened?" Dorothy cried out, rushing towards her mother. Her throat was dry with fear, her knees quivering as she closed the distance between them.

Her mother smiled easily and shook her head. "Dorothy Bowman, calm down. You're no banshee, dochder." Her laughter made Dorothy's nerves ease back instantly.

"I'm sorry, when I saw the car, I just thought…" Dorothy said breathlessly.

"You thought wrong. Kumm, help your daed," her mother said with a wink as she walked around the car.

The driver opened the other door and Dorothy's heart skipped a beat. For a moment, she remembered the day her father had fallen and how she had feared his demise. He might not be back to full health or ready to do everything he had done before, but he was finally home.

Tears welled in her eyes as she helped her father out of the car. He was lingering with a walking stick as an aid, but he was moving. He was back on his feet, Dorothy thought gratefully as she took the bags from the driver.

She followed her parents inside and relief washed over her as her father sat down in his favorite chair by the window. The nightmare was finally over. He was finally home and all better.

"Daed," Dorothy said once they settled him. "I'm so happy to see you're better."

Her father sighed heavily. "My health might be better, but I have a gut feeling my businesses are all backwards and upside down after my absence."

Dorothy ignored the sting of distrust and kept her smile in place. "They're just fine. We can go over the ledgers in the morning. Why don't we get you settled in first? Would you like me to cook your favorite dinner? Chicken pie and peas?"

"Nee, after your aunt sent it to the hospital every second day for the last six weeks, I doubt I'll ever be able to stomach it again," her father all but grunted.

It felt as if a tidal wave had just flooded their house, bringing with it negativity and ungratefulness. Dorothy had realized the type of man her father was when she had taken care of his businesses. She just hadn't realized he was like that towards everyone. If the last six weeks had helped her see more clearly, her vision was now twenty-twenty.

Her father was an entitled, ungrateful, and mean person who disregarded everyone else, regardless of their efforts to help him.

She drew in a deep breath. "Soup or stew?"

"Doesn't matter," her father mumbled. "Now, bring me my ledgers."

Her mother's hand gently rested on Dorothy's shoulder. Dorothy didn't have to meet her gaze to know that her mother was begging her to be patient. "I'll start dinner Dorothy. You bring your daed his ledgers."

Dorothy nodded before she collected the ledgers from the dining room table. She couldn't help but feel nervous when she returned to the living room to show her father what had happened in his absence.

"Her you go, Daed," Dorothy said, handing him everything except for the calculations she had made on a fresh sheet of paper. "I tried to record everything like you asked."

"Jah, but if you did it right, is the real question. I'm sure they had their fingers in the cash register and the bakery is probably running short on flour." He began muttering. "The gift shop probably kept the lights on just to spite me. Fools, all of them, ferhoodled fools!" her father all but cried out as he opened the first ledger.

Dorothy kept her silence, although deep down, she was brewing with anger at her father's attitude. The people he spoke of so badly were good people that worked long hard hours for him and instead of being grateful for their efforts, he allowed his suspicions to get the better of him.

Her father frowned when he started on the ledger for the gift shop. Dorothy watched his fingers slide over the numbers she had written in before he took the bank statement to see if they were correct. He gave her a curious look before he did the same with the other two businesses. When he was done, he shook his head before giving Dorothy a narrowed look.

"What is this? Are you lying to me?" her father's words felt like acid as he tossed it in her direction.

She stood up and for the first time knew that she might go against the ten commandments. "Nee Daed, I am not lying to you. I simply made a few changes, and that is the result. Here is a comparison between the last six weeks and the same six weeks the year before. As you can see, the money is in the bank. I'm not lying about anything," Dorothy whispered.

Her father snatched the page from her hand and went over the comparison. "But…" He looked up, his eyes narrowed with suspicion. "What did you do?"

Dorothy had been waiting for this moment and now she couldn't be sure if she had the courage to say what she needed to say. "I didn't… I trusted them. I treated them with kindness and thanked them for their hard work. I allowed the bakery to add some items to the menu, because customers were tired of the same products. I allowed the gift shop to take in more local crafts and I implemented weekly specials at the feed store."

Her father's eyes narrowed even as his face flushed red. "You…you… I asked you to oversee the businesses, Dorothy, not to reinvent the wheel. How could you discount items, add new inventory… this is…"

Before her father could allow his outburst to continue, her mother interrupted. "That's enough business for one evening, Eli. Dorothy, denke for everything you did. Your daed and I truly appreciate your efforts and I'm sure in the morning he'll be in a better mood and will be eager to hear how you increased the profits."

Her father was about to speak when her mother cast him a firm look. It was the first time in her life that Dorothy saw her mother standing up to her father.

Not another word was spoken about the businesses for the rest of the night, but when Dorothy finally climbed into bed, she couldn't help but feel as if a few things had changed while her father was in the hospital.

For one, she had learned the true nature of his personality.

Chapter 14
When Disguises Fail

The following morning, Caleb was relieved to hear that Eli was home. Although he knew his employer didn't hold him in high regard, Caleb still respected him from a distance. He also knew that Eli's return home would ease the load on Dorothy's shoulders, and she could let go of the constant worry over her father.

After he had finished the morning chores and taken care of everything he knew needed to be done, he headed to the farmhouse. It was a little after eleven in the morning and it felt strange to know that all the Bowmans were home.

Before the accident Eli would've been in town, and over the last few weeks, this was the time of morning that Dorothy usually went to town. He washed his hands by the pump and took a moment to wash his face as well before he headed up the porch.

As a child he would've thought nothing of going into the farmhouse, but as an adult he learned his place and his place wasn't in the big house, instead it was in the hidden cottage at the edge of the property.

"Caleb, what a pleasant surprise. How have you been?" Mrs. Bowman said, opening the door before he could even knock.

Caleb smiled warmly at the kind lady. He often wondered how she was so kind when her husband could be so mean? "Welcome home Mrs. Bowman. How have you been?"

"Very gut denke. Just glad to be home. Kumm in. Eli is probably itching to talk to you," Mrs. Bowman said, leading him into the living room.

For a moment Caleb allowed himself to remember having tea with Dorothy on the porch, but quickly pushed the thought aside as guilt washed over him. If Mr. Bowman knew how much time he and Dorothy had spent together, he wouldn't be talking about the farm at all this morning, instead Caleb and his parents would look for a new home.

He took off his hat and smiled as he entered the living room. "Welcome home Mr. Bowman."

Eli looked up, a disappointed frown already in place. "Guten mayrie Eli. Take a seat. Sarah, I'll take some kaffe, Caleb won't be staying long so need to make him any."

Caleb ignored the jab, hoping that by some miracle Eli realized the error of his ways after his accident.

Caleb forced a smile as he turned to Mr. Bowman. The last few weeks he had tried everything within his power to prove that he could run the farm and a worthy suitor for Dorothy. Now he had one chance to make Eli Bowman realize that. "Mr. Bowman, I think you'll be happy to see…"

"Happy? Why would I be happy? I end up in the hospital and without me looking over your shoulder, you've barely done anything at all. Do you think I didn't notice that the south field isn't plowed yet? Or that the fence is hanging in the western corner again? What about the weeds growing around the barn? I knew I couldn't trust you and you just proved it to me. You want to be a farm manager like your father, but you can hardly manage a few acres without having me nudging you in the right direction!"

Eli's voice was harsh, his eyes cold as he spoke in a low tone. For once he wasn't shouting at Caleb, but his quiet scolding was much more terrifying.

"But Mr. Bowman, I can explain about the south field, the rain..." Caleb began, hoping he would still have time to turn things around.

"Don't blame the rain. Only a fool blames the rain for his incompetence. You're probably going to tell me the chickens are to blame for the weeds as well!" Eli shouted this time.

Sarah walked into the living room, her head hanging low as she brought her husband his coffee.

"Eli, please..." she pleaded quietly.

"Nee. What for? He insists he's a farmer, but he can't even farm. I'm tired of being taken advantage of, I'm tired of..."

Before Eli could continue, Dorothy walked into the living room. "Daed!"

Caleb turned, relieved to see her, but feeling his heart clench at the pained look in her eyes. He wasn't sure if her father had treated her the same way regarding her handling of the businesses, but at that moment, he could see her disappointment in her father. Caleb wished he could shield her, but it was clearly too late.

There was nothing left to disguise Eli Bowman's true nature from a daughter that had admired him her whole life.

Chapter 15
A Daughter's Honesty

Dorothy had been about to leave for town when she heard her father shouting at Caleb. In the past she would've escaped her father's wrath, but she wasn't the same person she had been before his accident.

Looking back now, she had always assumed her father's anger was deserved, now she knew it wasn't. Especially not in Caleb's case. She stood in the living room doorway, both her parents looking at her with surprised bafflement in their eyes. Caleb's eyes held a warning for her not to get involved, but Dorothy was done standing by while her father battered people with his temper and hard words.

"Dorothy, I thought you were leaving?" her mother asked, almost as if warning her to go before her father turned his anger on her.

Dorothy shook her head and took a few steps into the room. "Nee. I'm not going before Daed apologizes to Caleb."

"What? Why should I apologize? He's the one that hasn't been doing his work!" her father cried out with rage.

Dorothy refused to raise her voice. She glanced at Caleb and rose her chin just enough to exude confidence. "He did more than any farm manager would've done in your absence. Regardless of how you treat him, he kept working while you were in the hospital. Do you know he barters labor to repair our fences and roofs because you refuse to buy new fence posts or roof shingles? Do you know he works on friends' farms over weekends, to get some much-needed help for the more difficult tasks? You might act like he does nothing, but you're hardly home enough to see how much he does."

Her father's face turned the color of a ripe tomato and Dorothy knew that when he exploded, she wouldn't get a word in edge wise, taking another breath, she continued.

"Last night you told me I changed everything; I reinvented the wheel on your businesses. I had to. You treated the people with such mistrust and condemnation that your suspicions in them created a dislike for our family. On the first day, everyone treated me as if I were about to let them go, or worse, scold them. Not one manager of your stores deserves such treatment. They are honest and hardworking and after showing them a little support and trust, they've made your businesses more successful. The way you treat people, it's wrong, Daed. It's not the way you taught me. You taught me that kindness is worth more than a week's wages. You taught that a gentle word can make a willful horse calm, yet you rule this community with suspicion, anger and cruelty. I never knew who you really were until now, Daed, and it hurts me to say that I'm disappointed. For the first time in my life, I'm ashamed to be your dochder." Dorothy had to bite back the tears as emotion flooded her voice. "This community is our family, Daed, and you treat them as if they are all stealing from you. Worldly possessions are a source of vanity, greed, and

Hochmuth, and yet it's all you care about. How can you expect me to live according to the ordnung, when you've long since forgotten what it contains?"

"Dorothy, hush. You can't talk to your daed like that," her mother urged by her side.

But her father's face had paled. With shock or shame, Dorothy couldn't be sure. "I have to, Mamm. Because no one else dares to stand up to him. Everyone depends on him either for employment or for feed or for their baking and they have kept quiet long enough. It's time Daed learned you can't treat people like this. It's not right. They're not deserving of his constant suspicion and wrath, especially not Caleb."

"I…" Caleb glanced at Dorothy. She could see he was trying to protect her, but she didn't need his protection. She knew her father was wrong, and in her heart, she knew Gott would want him to change his ways. She shook her head. "Caleb, I'm sure you have work you need to get on with."

Caleb frowned before he nodded. "Of course. I'll hitch the buggy for you."

"Nee, I won't be going into town today. Denke Caleb. I trust they will manage the stores just fine."

Dorothy waited until Caleb left before she moved towards her father. She kneeled before him and took his hands in hers. She searched his gaze and prayed that he would understand that she was being brutally honest because she cared, not because she wanted to hurt him like he hurt others. "Daed… they fear you. Can't you see you hurt them by treating them with suspicion? I showed you the ledgers, Daed. You can do the calculations again. No one is stealing from you. They're working harder than ever before *for* you."

Her father didn't say a word, instead he shook his head and let go of her hands. He turned his gaze out the window and Dorothy knew she was dismissed. When she stood up and turned, she saw the look on her mother's face.

She had gone too far.

But Dorothy couldn't regret it. She might have found kinder words, but she couldn't stand by and listen to her father scold Caleb when he'd done absolutely nothing wrong. She turned and glanced at her father one last time. "I love you, Daed. I know you're not this person. I know you're better."

Her father didn't make a sound or move, instead he kept completely still as he steadfastly looked out the window.

Chapter 16
Leopards Don't Change Their Spots

Caleb closed the door behind him and, for a moment, wished he could've stayed inside. He knew Dorothy had tried to protect him against her father, but he didn't need her protection.

Instead, he had to stop himself from rushing back inside to protect her against her father's wrath. He couldn't imagine that Eli Bowman would quietly sit by and listen while his daughter pointed out all his shortcomings.

He knew it had to be done, and he knew Dorothy was the right person to do it, but he just wished it didn't have to have been her. Dorothy was kind and sweet and he hated she had to stand up to her father. Caleb knew that although her voice had been calm and she had spoken with reason, her hands had quivered. They had quivered because she had felt as if she were betraying her father by telling him the truth.

The truth that the entire community accepted, even the bishop, but was too afraid to address. Knowing that eavesdropping would be out of the question, Caleb jogged down the stairs of the porch and crossed the yard to the barn.

He couldn't help but feel hopeless after what had just happened. Although Dorothy had come to his defense, it meant nothing for his cause. He'd wanted to prove to Eli that he was a capable and reliable man. Instead, Eli didn't even notice what he had done. He had merely pointed out what had yet to be done.

Caleb kicked the dust, wondering if he would ever demonstrate his true character to Eli. If he didn't have the opportunity, he knew that his feelings for Dorothy wouldn't ever matter. He had secretly hoped that after earning Eli's approval today that he could court Dorothy, but Eli's hard words had just clarified that he would never be good enough for Dorothy.

Whether or not he loved her.

He was just about to round the barn when he heard footsteps behind him. He turned and saw Dorothy rushing towards him from the house. For a brief moment, Caleb considered opening his arms and giving her the support he knew she needed after what she had just done.

"I'm so sorry Caleb… I didn't mean to interfere… I just couldn't listen to him scold you after everything you have done," Dorothy explained when she reached him.

"It's all right, denke," Caleb said, searching her gaze. He could see she was emotional after the confrontation. "It was very brave of you."

"Brave? I don't think he'll ever speak to me again," Dorothy admitted quietly. "But I couldn't hold my silence a moment longer. Last night he accused me of lying to him

about the profits and now this morning when he started on
you…"

"Dorothy, it's all right. He'll forgive you; you know he
cares for you very much," Caleb assured her, touching her
elbow.

Dorothy sighed. "That might be true, but why can't he
care for anyone else? Why can't he see how much you…" she
cut herself off just in time, but Caleb couldn't help but feel
hopeful at what she was about to say.

"I hoped he would see as well," Caleb finished for her
quietly. "But leopards don't change their spots."

Dorothy sighed, glancing at the cottage. "We're not
different, you and I. We're still the same, although we're no
longer friends…"

"I thought we were friends again?" Caleb asked gently.

There was so much unsaid between them he wasn't even
sure where to start. "Dorothy, just know this. I'm grateful for
what you just did. No one else has ever defended me before.
I want you to know how much it means to me to know that
you… care."

Her smile was weak as she met his gaze. "It means a lot
to me to know that you care as well."

"At least that won't ever change," Caleb finished, letting
his hand slide from her elbow to her hand.

For a moment they just stood there, appreciating each
other and accepting the reality that they could never speak
freely about their feelings to each other. Eli had created a
vast crevice between them that could only be crossed by his
blessing, one that both Caleb and Dorothy knew they would
never have.

Caleb squeezed her hand and prayed silently that one day Gott would give him the courage to ask for Dorothy's hand, for Eli's blessing to court the girl he had always loved. He knew he had little to offer, but he had his heart, and he knew for the type of woman that Dorothy was, that would be more than enough.

A tear slipped over her cheek, and she quickly brushed it away. "I have to get back... go into town..."

"Jah," Caleb agreed, although neither of them moved. "Dorothy... you're a gut woman. Never let anyone, not even your daed, make you doubt that."

Dorothy's smile was tearful as she nodded. "Denke Caleb. You're a gut man, a gut farmer, and a hard worker, and don't let my daed make you doubt that. I'll understand if you choose to leave instead of continuing to work for him. Don't worry about your parents, I'll make sure he doesn't turn them away."

Caleb's heart swelled in his chest, knowing that she meant it. She would let him go to let him find happiness and she would care for his parents, although she didn't owe them anything. It made him love her even more. "Not today... I'm not leaving today."

Dorothy nodded. "Just promise me that if you do... you'll say gut bye?"

Caleb smiled. "Of course. A friend that cares will never leave without saying gut bye."

Their gazes held for a few moments longer before Dorothy sighed and headed back to the house. Caleb watched her walk away and wondered how much longer he was going to stay on the farm, hoping her father would finally give his blessing.

A leopard didn't change his spots, and he doubted that Eli Bowman would ever change the way he looked at Caleb and his family.

Chapter 17
Rebirth

No one spoke of that morning again.

The following morning, her father had simply asked if she would continue visiting the stores in town as she had been doing while he had been in the hospital. Her father hadn't explained his reasoning or even told her when he'd be taking over again and Dorothy didn't ask.

There was a dark cloud hanging over their home, one ripe with the truth that Dorothy had confronted her father with. While Dorothy continued to tend to the businesses, her father sat in his chair by the window watching Caleb work for most of the time.

Her mother quickly fell back into her routine of housekeeping and cooking, having more work now with Dorothy spending most of her mornings in town. Whereas Dorothy was glad to have her mother home and to know her father felt better, it felt as if the air was slowly suffocating her.

Not even over dinner was their conversation comfortable, only more of that deafening silence that Dorothy hated.

A few times, she had considered apologizing to her father. But apologizing to him would mean that Dorothy was wrong and that he'd been right, and he hadn't been right. For that reason only, Dorothy kept her silence as well. Over the last few sleepless nights she had consulted Gott's word many times and every time she found more scriptures confirming that her father's treatment of people had been wrong and that it was her duty as a fellow member of the congregation to bring him back into Gott's fold of faith and kindness.

It had been the hardest thing she had ever done and even now, as she arrived home from town; she knew it would become harder still.

Her father wasn't one to forgive easily, and after the way she had confronted him with the truth in front of both Caleb and her mother, she doubted he would ever forgive her.

Dorothy had also read in the bible that as a daughter she shouldn't hang onto resentments and instead she should believe in her father and in Gott's strength. At the moment, that was the only reason she kept working, kept praying, and kept hoping that somehow her father's heart would change.

She walked into the house and set down her ledgers on the living room table when she heard voices in the living room.

Men's voices.

For a moment, she considered scurrying to the kitchen to give them the privacy they deserved, but her curiosity made her turn in that direction instead. Laughter drifted in the air as she stopped in the doorway.

Dorothy frowned, wondering if she was hallucinating or if she had arrived at the wrong house.

Caleb sat on a chair, cupping a mug of coffee between his hands, laughing at something her father had said. Her mother sat on the armrest of her father's chair, joining in the laughter. Her eyes narrowed, certain that she was imagining it, when her father's voice broke through her thoughts.

"Dorothy, kumm join us." Her father beckoned her closer with a smile. For a moment, Dorothy was reminded of the snake in the garden of Eden and hesitated.

"Kumm dochder. Sarah, pour her a cup of kaffe, please. She deserves to rest for a bit after all the back and forth she does into town and back," Eli said with a jubilant smile.

Dorothy glanced at her mother, wondering who the stranger was that had taken the shape of her father. Her mother stopped in front of her and smiled. "Denke. Denke for bringing back the mann I fell in love with."

Even more confused, Dorothy took a seat. Her back was ramrod straight, as if ready to flee at any moment as she glanced at Caleb.

Caleb smiled with an easy shrug before he took a sip of his coffee.

"We've been waiting for you to return," her father said with a kind smile. "There's something I need to talk to you about."

"I've got to check on a few things," Caleb said, putting down his cup.

"Nee, nee. Please stay Caleb. You were here when my dochder pointed out the error of my ways, so it's only right if you hear me apologize," Eli said easily, gesturing Caleb to stay.

Dorothy's heart . She couldn't help but feel as if her father had lured her into a trap.

"Dochder, last week when you said those things, I never realized I could become so angry, so resentful of my own blood. I was certain that you had turned against me, just like my employees, Caleb, and the rest of the community." Her father let out a heavy sigh. "It took a lot of contemplation, introspection, and patience to come to accept that you were right. No one turned on me, Dorothy, I turned my back on my faith and on the rest of the world."

Dorothy couldn't stop her jaw from dropping. "Daed?"

Her father chuckled softly. "I've spent the last week trying to figure out where I changed, how I became so suspicious, and eventually realized it's not the past that matters but the future. I have to make amends; I have to apologize to so many people for my behavior. But I first had to make things right with Gott."

Dorothy glanced at Caleb again, not sure if her ears were hearing correctly. "You did?"

"Jah, and after I did, I knew that making amends had to start at home. I've apologized to your mamm and now it's time for me to apologize to you. I'm sorry that you had to see that side of me. I'll be forever grateful that you had the courage to confront me about it. Denke for everything you've done these last few weeks, denke for being… the best dochder a daed could ask for." Eli's voice broke with emotion.

Dorothy realized it wasn't a dream or her imagination as her mother placed a cup of coffee in her hands. "He's apologized to Caleb as well."

"You did?" Dorothy asked her father before she turned to Caleb. "He did?"

Caleb nodded, but didn't say a word.

"Jah. Over these last few days, I've realized how much Caleb does without being asked, how much he cares for the farm. And today when I apologized, I came to know the type of man he is." Her father grinned at Caleb and shook his head. "A kind but stubborn one, it turns out."

Dorothy shook her head, confused. "Stubborn?"

"Jah." Her father nodded with a chuckle. "I apologized to him for asking him to stay away from you when he turned sixteen. I apologized for my behavior over the years, my treatment of him... for so many things and he refused to accept my apology without one condition."

"Condition?" Dorothy felt as if she was a parrot. Struggling to comprehend how much was happening.

"He would only accept my apology if I gave him my blessing to court you – that is if you wish to be courted by him."

Her heart stopped for a moment as she turned to Caleb and saw his mouth curve into an amiable smile. She turned to her father and shrugged. "I don't know what to say..."

Her mother's laughter rang in the air. "Tell your daed you forgive him and tell Caleb you wish for him to court you."

Dorothy couldn't find the words. Instead, she just nodded as joy spread through her being and overflowed with tears of happiness. She glanced around the room and suddenly the dark cloud was gone.

The anger, the resentment, and the negativity had disappeared as the grace of God shone through the window with beams of light, chasing away the darkness for good.

Epilogue

Dorothy stood in the cornfield and smiled up at the sun. Nothing brought her more joy than to feel the sun on her skin, feel the fresh air rejuvenate her lungs, and know that Gott had blessed her with all this and more.

She would always find simple pleasures on the farm and all it offered, but over the last six months she enjoyed the challenges running a business offered. After her father had found his faith again, he had insisted that it was time for him to spend more time with her mother. He had retired and handed over the reins of all three businesses to Dorothy without a single condition or warning.

Dorothy now ran the bakery, the gift shop, and the feed store completely on her own and enjoyed every second. Just like she enjoyed learning more about business, her employees enjoyed having her as their new boss.

Her father had made amends with everyone he had wronged and had gone above and beyond with Caleb's parents. Instead of just apologizing for making them feel inferior all those years, he had subdivided the land and was putting the cottage section into their names, so that they knew they would never have to find a new home again.

And as for her and Caleb, not even in her dreams had she been so happy.

After her father gave his blessing for them to court, they had attended Sunday singings. It punctuated their buggy rides with the most interesting conversations about everything from thoughts on farming to their dreams of the future.

Over the holidays, Caleb and his family had joined them at the farmhouse and had celebrated the special days with them as a family. Although they had always lived apart from each other on the farm, Dorothy finally acknowledged that was what they were. In their own way, they had always been family.

When her father had retired at first, Dorothy had feared that his stepping back from the businesses would mean he was going to micromanage the farm. Looking over Caleb's shoulder at every turn. But he had put complete faith in Caleb and except for a weekly update on what was happening on the farm, he hardly ever questioned Caleb's judgment at all.

Dorothy glanced up at the cloudless sky, remembering that just a few months ago, as autumn turned to winter, she had thought Caleb would leave and that her father would never speak to her again. But now, as spring turned to summer, she knew Gott was a God of miracles. He could bring the cold and create a barren landscape of ghostly arms and snowy fields, freezing away every sign of life. And then, as if by miracle, the weather would change, the snow would melt, and the soil would be fertile to give birth to new life.

A contented sigh escaped her, knowing that it was by a gracious merciful miracle of Gott that her father had changed. That he found the right path again, and that he had allowed her to find joy with Caleb. She had never known what love would feel like, but as Dorothy smiled up at the sun, she could almost compare it with that feeling.

A sensation enveloping your whole body knowing that you were accepted, loved, and cherished.

"Are you hiding from me in the cornfield?" Caleb's voice suddenly asked behind her.

Dorothy laughed as she turned to meet his gaze. "Not at all. I'm soaking up at the sun. I brought you lunch," she pointed to the basket at her feet. "I finished earlier in town than I thought."

"So I have the privilege of enjoying lunch with you? How about we go sit under the tree over there by the fence line? She knew exactly which tree he meant. It was the one that gave them a view of the entire farm.

"Perfect."

They ate apples and grapes, drunk juice and water, and laughed about trivial things like an ant trying to carry a twig that was almost a hundred times its size. Dorothy knew it was wrong to be grateful for her father's accident, but how could she not be when it had brought her joy and had brought her father to be the man she always thought him to be?

"I was hoping I'd see you today. I wanted to ask you something," Caleb said, interrupting her thoughts.

"Jah, I already said I'd be around for the harvest," Dorothy laughed. Ever since he had planted the corn fields, it was barely all he could talk about.

"Actually, I wanted to ask you something else," Caleb said heavily.

Dorothy frowned, wondering what he had on his mind. She waited patiently for him to continue.

When he took her hand and gently pressed a kiss over her fingers, her heart raced with love.

"Dorothy, with your daed's blessing, I want to ask if you'd spend the rest of your life with me?" Caleb's mouth curved into a grin.

Dorothy gasped. "Caleb, are you proposing?"

Caleb laughed. "If you ask, I must be doing it wrong. Dorothy, would you be my frau until Gott calls us home? Will you spend your life with me on this farm, will you be the mother of my kinner and grow old with me?"

If the day could've been any more perfect, Dorothy didn't know how. She beamed at Caleb and felt her future unfold before her with more love and joy than she could've ever asked for. "Jah, of course I will."

Caleb returned her loving smile with a cheeky grin. "Gut, because after asking your daed, I was terrified you'd say nee."

Their laughter travelled on the breeze as looked towards the future together.

*** The End ***

Thank you kindly for choosing to read my book. I sincerely hope you enjoyed it. All of my Amish Romances are wholesome stories suitable for all to enjoy.

If you could be so kind to leave a review on Amazon, I would appreciate it.